Rock Solid

Rock Solid

By James Preller

SCHOLASTIC INC.
New York   Toronto   London   Auckland   Sydney
Mexico City   New Delhi   Hong Kong

No part of this work may be reproduced, stored in a retrieval system, or transmitted in any form or by any means, electronic, mechanical, photocopying, recording, or otherwise, without written permission of the publisher. For information regarding permission, write to Scholastic Inc., Attention: Permissions Department, 555 Broadway, New York, NY 10012.

ISBN 0-439-23525-1
Design by Joan Moloney

Copyright © 2000 Scholastic Inc. All rights reserved. Published by Scholastic Inc. SCHOLASTIC and associated logos are trademarks and/or registered trademarks of Scholastic Inc.

12 11 10 9 8 7 6 5 4 3 2 1   0 1 2 3 4 5 6/0

Printed in the U.S.A.
First Scholastic printing, July 2000

Dedicated to the memory of my first wrestling hero, Gorilla Monsoon.

And to my old friend Peter Mameli, college professor and wrestling fan, who dragged me to the first WrestleMania closed-circuit broadcast long ago in a galaxy far, far away.

And lastly, to The Rock, without whom this book would be incredibly short.

TABLE OF CONTENTS

1

Introduction   1

2

The Family Business   4

3

Breaking the Illusion   9

4

Coming Out a Winner   14

5

High School   17

6

A Miami Hurricane   21

7

Heartbreak   25

8

Turning Point   29

9

Selling the Show   32

10

Wrestling School   34

11
The Survivor   38

12
Heels and Baby Faces   41

13
Trouble Cooking   44

14
Die, Rocky, Die   47

15
Birth of The Rock   51

16
All Too Real   56

17
Talking the Talk   60

18
Mankind   64

19
A Heel of a Thing to Do   69

20
Greatness   74

21
The Rock and Sock Combination   77

22
Next? The World!   81

Rock Solid

CHAPTER 1
Introduction

The music starts. Like an electrical charge, a volt of excitement ripples through the arena. "DO YOU SMELL WHAT THE ROCK IS COOKING?"

Thump, ba-thump. THUMP, BA-THUMP. The bass beat kicks in, bringing the crowd to its feet. And there he is, all 275 magnificent pounds of him, raising an eyebrow over a pair of designer shades at the cheering crowd. As if The Rock cares one way or another. Love him, hate him, *whatever*. It's all the same to The Rock.

He's just arrived to lay the smack down on whatever roody-poo jabroni dares get in the ring with him. He's a fierce competitor. The Rock shows absolutely no fear and will face whatever opponent is thrown his way. Be it the monstrous Big Show, the indestructible Undertaker, or even treacherous Triple H. The Rock will serve a shot of shut-up juice to anyone unfortunate enough to be in his ring. The People's ring.

And because of that *attitude* — his magnetic charisma, his monumental arrogance, his flashy style (catch that Rolex watch and five-hundred-dollar shirt), and his over-the-top ego — the fans adore him.

But The Rock doesn't care. He's heard 'em boo. He's heard 'em cheer. No big thing. The Rock knows his role. He goes out and fights hard — and The Rock means *hard* — and puts on one heck of an entertaining show. Every single night. That's what made him The People's Champion.

Win or lose, belt or no belt, it doesn't matter. Because The Rock keeps rocking. He'll whip 'em all in the ring, too. There's no stopping The Rock. He's destined to become the big kahuna. Like a hit single from Elvis, he's number one and *still* rising.

And the crowd goes *wild* for him — the self-proclaimed "most electrifying man in sports entertainment." He's a hulk of a man with a gift for gab, self-confidence by the boatload, and attitude to burn. A man who talks the talk. And talks some more. A man with the talent and the jaw-dropping athleticism to back up every word.

This is the story of how he reached the top. And how a nation of fans — the millions . . . *and millions* — began to shout his name. How he turned the doubts and jeers into deafening cheers.

This is the story of how a boy named Dwayne Johnson grew up to become The Rock.

JABRONI

The Rock popularized this phrase in the promotional announcements he made for the World Wrestling Federation (WWF). But he didn't invent the term. In fact, it's an insider phrase used in the world of professional wrestling. It means a nothing, a nobody. Two other versions of this phrase are "jobber" and "ham-and-egger." But could you imagine The Rock saying anything but jabroni? If The Rock calls you a jabroni, well, sorry, but you've just been dissed.

CHAPTER 2
The Family Business

You can't talk about Dwayne Johnson, a.k.a. The Rock, without talking about his father, Rocky Johnson. And once you talk about Rocky, then you've pretty much got to mention Dwayne's *grand*father, High Chief Peter Maivia.

Both men were professional wrestlers. More than that, both men were title-holders. Heavyweight champions. Big, powerful, no-nonsense guys. Tough as leather and harder than concrete. Peter Maivia, father of Dwayne's mother, Ata, held the most honored title in the Samoan community: Paramount High Chief. He dedicated his life to professional wrestling, first as a wrestler and later as a promoter, organizing shows all throughout the South Pacific.

Peter Maivia stood five feet, ten inches. A pure Samoan warrior, he weighed 320 pounds. Later in life, Peter would have his body covered in traditional Samoan tattoos.

And so that was the world into which Dwayne Johnson was born on May 2, 1972. A world of suplexes and piledrivers, screaming fans and forearm shivers. Wrestling, you see, was the family business for Dwayne Johnson.

There wasn't a moment when wrestling wasn't in Dwayne's life. It was normal, like breathing air. Except the air he breathed smelled like sweat socks and moldy mats. When his grandfather's friends stopped by to visit, they were wrestling superstars of that era, including Andre the Giant and Ric Flair. And, when the over seven-

WRESTLE-MANIA III: THE GREATEST FINALE

The final match to WrestleMania III provided perhaps the single most memorable image in wrestling history. In the main event, seven-foot, four-inch Andre the Giant challenged his former friend and current title-holder, Hulk Hogan, to a championship match. Though Hulk was the champion and beloved by fans everywhere, Andre the Giant was a potent threat — he had never lost a match. Incredibly, toward the end of a brutal battle, Hulk Hogan lifted the five hundred-plus pound Giant into the air — and slammed him to the canvas! Fans gasped in shock. It had never been seen before. One, two, three, pin. The fans who had packed the Pontiac Silverdome in Michigan — all 93,173 of them — erupted. The Giant had been slain.

foot five-hundred-pound Andre stopped by for dinner, the Maivias had to have plenty of food on hand!

Dwayne's earliest memories involved wrestling. While other kids may have daydreamed about Superman or Batman, Dwayne had his own larger-than-life hero — a guy called Dad. Dwayne would often accompany his mother to watch Rocky's matches. The crowd, the excitement, the showmanship, the noise — Dwayne loved it all.

Rocky Johnson, Dwayne's father, was tall, dark, and handsome. Rocky had the look, all right. He also had the skills. Rocky was a gifted gymnast, able to execute powerful and graceful moves in the ring. He carried himself with dignity and poise. He was, in a word, *proud*. Fans could see that — and they respected him for it. Rocky Johnson was a good guy and a class act.

He broke barriers, too. Rocky was the first African-American to win the World Wrestling Federation Intercontinental title. Later in his career, in 1983, he teamed with Tony Atlas to become the first African-American tag team to hold the WWF World Tag-Team Championship belt.

Rocky Johnson began his wrestling career in the

early 1960s. It was a different era then. Wrestling was not the entertainment powerhouse it is today. It offered a good living, no doubt. But it was a hard life. There were no pay-per-view shows or lucrative merchandising deals. Being a professional wrestler was like belonging to a traveling theater troupe. The wrestlers would set up in different regions, working in a particular territory for a period of weeks or months. Then they'd move on to a new territory before the fans grew bored of seeing the same guys over and over.

Dwayne was born in Haywood, California, but by the time he'd reached kindergarten, he'd lived in five different states. At age eight, he moved again — to Hawaii. But that was no problem for Dwayne. He liked the new places and faces. Even better, in Hawaii Dwayne got to spend time with his maternal grandparents, Peter and Leah. He felt truly at home.

Growing up (and growing, and GROWING!), Dwayne would often pretend he was a wrestler, performing dropkicks on imaginary opponents. And sometimes, when no one was looking, Dwayne would take out his father's championship belt. He'd hold it, touch it lightly with his fingers, and pose with it slung over his shoulder. He'd stand up tall, arms stretched and triumphantly hold the belt over his head.

The new World Wrestling Federation Champion — little Dwayne Johnson!

CHAPTER 3
Breaking the Illusion

From an early age, Dwayne understood the world of wrestling. He knew it was an act, or, as insiders called it, *a work* — a creative performance with planned outcomes. His father never pretended otherwise. Though Rocky Johnson was immensely proud of his career in the ring, he was equally proud of his craft: the *art* of his performance, his very real athletic ability.

However, most of the viewing population did not have the advantage of Dwayne's behind-the-scenes knowledge. Many did not fully realize that before entering the ring, each wrestler knew who was going to win, and who was going to lose. The only thing the wrestlers didn't know, of course, was exactly *how* it would happen. That was their job, making it all seem convincing *and* entertaining for the audience.

Selling it. They did a great job of confusing the audience.

Once upon a time, you couldn't discuss professional wrestling without hearing the same argument. "It's all fake," one person might contend. "No way! It's real!" the other would counter. The debate raged on, back and forth, endlessly.

Which is just the way professional wrestling wanted it. They had a strict code. A line that could not be crossed. *It was real — all of it —* they'd claim. Every bodyslam, every piledriver, every chair smashed over someone's head. Every staggering suplex, every brutal betrayal, every crazy character.

There was a time when the average fan did not realize that there were real people behind legendary (if somewhat cartoonish) characters such as The Iron Sheik, George "The Animal" Steele, or Gorgeous George. There was a time when *the secret* was guarded. No one betrayed the secret. Wrestling promoters feared that if the fans knew it was orchestrated, they would turn away from the shows. It was considered the highest crime, the worst of the worst, for anyone in the business to break the illusion.

In the beginning, professional wrestling was a real sport. But the amateur style and long matches left many spectators yawning. No one wanted to see two men grapple for an hour until one was pinned. By adding storylines and flamboyant characters and drama, wrestling became an addiction for many fans.

Now wrestling is openly called "sports entertainment," not an athletic competition. It's a work. An amazing, astonishing, athletic, incredible *show*. The characters are no more real than any character you would see in a movie. Real men born with ordinary names play all of the characters. Each character has an ever-changing role to play, with outrageous plotlines to follow. They have a show to put on.

The official break with the past came in the mid-1980s. That's when World Wrestling Federation officials publicly admitted to the New Jersey State Athletic Commission the "worked" nature of professional wrestling. They stated that what the company presents is *entertainment,* not a true athletic contest. This admission forced the state to remove the New Jersey Athletic Commission (and the fees and restrictions that went with it!) as a governing body of professional wrestling. In effect, they no longer viewed professional wrestling as a true sport. It was "sports entertainment."

A decade later, the A&E cable network featured a special called *The Unreal Story of Professional Wrestling*. In it, various wrestlers further admitted the truth, and gave details to support it. At the time, the program was the highest-rated special in the history of the A&E cable network. Nobody was kidding anybody anymore.

By giving up the illusion, the WWF and other wrestling organizations gained a degree of freedom. Plots and backstories could be wilder than ever. Today, pro wrestling — with action figures, video games, television contracts, advertising dollars, and pay-per-view specials — generates more money than ever.

And today's fans have access to vast amounts of information via the Internet, newsletters, and countless magazines. Professional wrestling doesn't just have fans. It has *critics* — people who review the show just as some might review a movie or a Broadway play.

Breaking the illusion was good for business. Yet in some respects, it didn't really matter one way or the other. Not to the fans. Because part of being a fan is, in the words of the poet Samuel Taylor

Coleridge, "the willing suspension of disbelief." That is, the fans aren't dumb. They know what's what. They are in on the con. But still, and here's the kicker, they *want* to be worked. So bring on the show — and don't forget the metal folding chairs!

DROPPING THE BELT IS . . .

Intentionally letting your opponent win in a title match.

In a title match, a belt can only change hands in the event of a pin or submission move (forcing your opponent to tap out). A title match ending in a disqualification or count out allows the defending champion to keep the belt.

CHAPTER 4
Coming Out a Winner

It would be years before young Dwayne Johnson would ever see action inside a professional ring. He had some growing up to do first — and it wasn't always easy.

When you're the biggest kid around, and when your father is a famous wrestler, people are going to notice you. And Dwayne accepted that. Deep down, he enjoyed it. But that kind of notoriety has its downside. Because for some teenagers, there's nothing quite so satisfying as beating the living snot out of the Big Kid.

By age thirteen, Dwayne had the body of a man. He weighed 170 pounds and stood six feet in thick socks. It's the kind of thing that draws attention. And if you're Dwayne Johnson, an exotic-looking kid with a dark temper who backs down from nobody, then you're going to have more than your fair share of fights.

Which was okay with Dwayne. He didn't mind fighting every so often. It was something to do. Not that he went out looking for fights, mind you. Dwayne's clear on that. It was just that he wasn't real good at walking away from trouble. When trouble came knocking, Dwayne Johnson knocked right back.

But one day it didn't work out so well.

Word went out that Billy, a sixteen-year-old, wanted a piece of Dwayne Johnson, three years his junior. Why? No reason, really. In fact, none at all — except that Dwayne was the son of a famous wrestler. Dwayne shrugged. Sure, he'd meet Billy after school. Why not?

Dwayne wasn't afraid of a fair fight.

But fair wasn't what Billy had in mind.

While Dwayne waited with his friend José in an arranged spot — a park across from the junior high — Billy showed up with more than twenty-five friends. You didn't need to be a genius to figure out the odds. Anybody could smell what was cooking. Dwayne was dead meat. José urged Dwayne to run while there was still a chance. But Dwayne refused.

ROCK WINS THE ROYAL RUMBLE 2000

The Royal Rumble was held at Madison Square Garden in New York City, January 23, 2000, involving thirty wrestlers. The rumble began with two wrestlers in the ring. Then, every sixty seconds, a new wrestler joined the battle. Once a wrestler was hurled over the top rope, he could not reenter the ring. The lone man left would be declared the winner. Well, The Rock looked it over, calculated the odds, and decided everything looked cool to him. He boldly predicted that he'd win (was there ever a fight he didn't think he'd win?). The man walked the walk, concluding the match by dramatically flipping a seven-foot, two-inch, five-hundred-pound behemoth named The Big Show over the ropes.

Some part of him still hoped for a fair fight. He still believed, despite all odds, he could take care of business.

To call it a fight would be unfair. It was a total assault, with Billy's gang blindsiding Dwayne at will, getting in kicks and punches, while Dwayne staggered around helplessly. The beating continued even after Dwayne fell to the ground and tried to protect himself from the blows.

Dwayne was dirtied, bloodied, but still unbroken. He wouldn't run. He wouldn't surrender. Billy and those guys — they couldn't take away Dwayne's pride. No one could. He may have lost an unfair fight. But he still came out a winner.

CHAPTER 5
High School

By the time Dwayne turned fifteen, he was six feet, four inches tall. He weighed 225 pounds. Thanks to countless hours in the gym, most of that weight was muscle.

Once again, Dwayne's family was on the move. When he landed in Bethlehem, Pennsylvania, for his sophomore year of high school, Dwayne had already lived in thirteen states — not to mention the counry of New Zealand.

For Dwayne, Freedom High School in Bethlehem was no big thing. He'd been the new guy before. He knew how to fit in and make new friends.

That's when, for one day, Dwayne Johnson gave wrestling a go. No, not professional wrestling. *Real* wrestling. The kind done in schools across America.

That is, the *sport* of wrestling — not the show. No backflips off the top rope. No sleeper holds or Samoan backdrops or crazy characters in face paint.

Curious, eager to fit in, Dwayne figured he'd check it out. Now understand, Dwayne Johnson knew *nothing* about amateur wrestling. He only knew it was real. So it was with some nervousness that Dwayne first entered Freedom's hot, cramped, smelly gym. After a few minutes, Dwayne was told to tangle with the team's leader, their number one heavyweight. The whistle blew and the match was over almost as quickly as it had begun. Dwayne wiped the floor with the heavyweight, easily defeating his opponent.

Now maybe that would mean something to most people. After all, it was quite an achievement. But Dwayne felt strangely unaffected by it. High school wrestling just didn't compare to the excitement of professional wrestling. To Dwayne, it was . . . *boring*.

Football was another story. Dwayne loved football. He liked memorizing plays and studying films. He enjoyed the tough practices and hard workouts. He was always struggling to contain his ferocious temper. Dwayne found in football the perfect outlet for his aggression. And he was good at it.

He played defensive end and tight end. By his junior year, Dwayne made all-conference. In his senior year, the colleges came calling, offering free scholarships if Dwayne would only agree to play ball at their school. Every day more recruiting mail reached his home. The phone rang constantly. Coaches traveled far and wide to visit. *Sign here*, they'd say. *Come to our school. You'll love it.*

Dwayne tore up the field that senior year, and was named high school All-America by *USA Today*. He was also named one of the top ten players in the state of Pennsylvania. And slowly, gradually, a new dream stirred within him.

He wanted to play in the NFL.

But first, he had to choose a college. From the beginning, Dwayne

The Rock Lays The Smack Down on — The Rock?!

Dwayne Johnson may have been the biggest, baddest, best-looking guy in Freedom High School, but he had his embarrassing moments, too. The Rock told *Teen People* magazine about the time he finished his SATs early. He sat at his desk, tapping his pencil and feeling confident, when, "Wham! My chair fell backwards, I hit the floor, and my feet flew up in the air. Everyone was laughing." You might think The Rock laid the smack down on those jabronis, but he played it cool. And he got a great score on the test!

19

knew one thing: It would have to be somewhere warm. Dwayne had endured enough of Pennsylvania's frozen winters. He finally settled on a school, one of the top programs in the nation — the University of Miami.

Dwayne Johnson was on the move again.

CHAPTER 6
A Miami Hurricane

In high school, Dwayne had always prided himself on his hard work. He poured his heart out on the football field. But the big-time college game — that was another story. It was hard, *hard* work. To Dwayne, as an eighteen-year-old freshman, it felt like he'd just joined the Marines. Coaches watched his every move, screaming in his ear throughout practice. After drills, the players would hit the hot, noisy weight room and lift weights until they collapsed with exhaustion.

It was the Hurricane way. A point of pride.

The game was rougher and more violent than in high school. And the players were a whole lot bigger. Still, Dwayne kept his mouth shut and knew his role. Through hard work and force of will, Dwayne impressed Head Coach Dennis Erickson. He rose above several older, more experienced players in the depth charts and, as a mere freshman, was listed as the second-string defensive tackle. It was no small feat. Especially when you consider that the first-string tackle was the great Russell Maryland, who would eventually go on to make quarterbacks miserable for the Dallas Cowboys.

About a week before the season opener, fate dealt Dwayne a lousy hand. He got hurt during practice. One moment, Dwayne was performing at his all-time best, a bright future there for the taking. Then in a terrible instant, it all changed. An illegal block brought Dwayne crashing to the ground. Suddenly Dwayne was eating turf, groaning in pain, trying hard not scream out in agony. It hurt so much, he could barely stay conscious, as the team trainer yanked at his arm, calmly trying to work it back into its socket. Dwayne later learned that he'd torn some ligaments and separated his shoulder. That meant surgery. And surgery meant that he'd be forced to miss the entire season.

It was a difficult, stressful time for Dwayne. He was away from home for the first time in his life. He no longer felt a part of the team. He didn't have a purpose, a meaningful role. He grew depressed; he missed his family. Soon he missed his classes, too, and his grades plummeted. Dwayne felt lost and uncertain. He wanted to give up, pack it in, and go home.

But there's something you need to know about Dwayne Johnson. No matter how bad things look, he's not a quitter. He saw his life spiraling out of control — and he vowed to turn it around. It wasn't easy, but he became a good student. And something else happened. He met Dany Garcia. She was, in Dwayne's eyes, everything he'd ever dreamed of in a woman: smart and beautiful, lively and intelligent. Like a bolt of lightning, Dwayne *knew* — without a glimmer of doubt — that this was the woman for him. Dwayne and Dany have been together ever since.

The next season, 1991, was officially Dwayne's freshman year as a football player, since he'd missed the entire previous season. The Hurricanes were unstoppable that season, going undefeated and winning the national championship. They were a tough, supremely talented, wildly arrogant group of athletes. And they didn't mind saying so. The Hurricanes practically invented Attitude with a capital "A."

In every game, they'd talk trash to their opponents. They'd brag about all the great things they were going to do — then they'd go out *and do them*. It was the Hurricane way. Dwayne Johnson watched, listened, and learned. And then he talked the trash, too. Those lessons would come in handy a few years later, when in front of packed arenas The Rock began to "lay the smack down" for all to hear.

CHAPTER 7
Heartbreak

Even with his success on the football field —
even as he poured heart and soul into becoming an
NFL football player — the idea of professional
wrestling still rumbled in the back of Dwayne's
mind. He didn't dare tell Dany, not yet anyway.
But it was always a possibility. Wouldn't it be cool
to follow his father, and his grandfather, into the
ring?

Dwayne Johnson had his finest college football
season in 1993, his junior year. He'd gotten his
grades up, too, and was working toward a degree in
criminology. It was a proud moment when he was
named academic captain of the team. He was a true
student-athlete.

The fiercest, best defensive tackle on the team? Sorry Dwayne, but you'll have to move over. Warren Sapp's in the house. Today, Warren eats quarterbacks for lunch on Sundays in the NFL — and he just might be the best man at his position. So it was all right with Dwayne when Warren, a sophomore, beat him out for the starting job. No disgrace in that, none at all. Besides, the system at Miami still gave Dwayne plenty of "snaps," or time on the field.

Dwayne felt healthy and confident. His body was strong, exploding with vitality and quickness. He was focused and falling in love with football all over again. He loved the locker room, the bond of friendship among teammates, the killer practices, and the thrill of Saturday games.

Things were definitely looking up.

By his senior year, it was obvious to everyone. Dwayne Johnson had a realistic shot at making the NFL. Several preseason polls even named him all-America in anticipation of his upcoming, monster season.

It never happened. Once again, his body betrayed him. During the first day of practice in pads, Dwayne charged an offensive lineman like a Brahma bull. He struck the lineman with a helmet, clean in the chest. Suddenly, crippling pain stabbed at Dwayne's lower back, shooting down both legs.

X-rays were ordered. Doctors poked and prodded him. Then they sat Dwayne down and gave it to him straight. He was facing a career-ending injury. Two disks in his back had badly ruptured. He might never play football again. Just like that, in an instant, Dwayne saw his college career headed for the trash heap.

Well, when you're built like Dwayne Johnson, that's not something you easily accept. He was tough. He was Rocky Johnson's son. Grandson of High Chief Peter Maivia. His body would bounce back; it always did. He just needed to suck it up. Fight through the pain. After all, he wasn't going to make the NFL by lying around on the couch, eating potato chips, and watching television.

So Dwayne practiced despite the doctors' advice. Which was okay with the coaching staff. Because that's football. How much could it hurt anyway? And wasn't Dwayne Johnson a tough guy? He could take it, right?

Dwayne fought on. He gave it his best, all he had, like always. But his body wasn't willing. He had a poor, painful, heartbreaking season. Dwayne had lost something along the way. A step here, a burst of energy there, a degree of pure power. He'd lost the razor edge that separates the good from the great.

When the NFL Draft came along, it passed right over Dwayne Johnson. Not a single team was willing to take a chance on a lineman with a bad back. Nobody, it felt to him, wanted Dwayne Johnson.

CHAPTER 8
Turning Point

Another thing about Dwayne Johnson — he doesn't let go of dreams easily. He'll keep coming, long after others would have quit. That's just the way he's made. So when an offer came in to try Canadian football in the CFL, Dwayne made the trip north to Alberta, Canada, and gave it one last effort.

The money was bad. The lifestyle was worse. Dwayne's bed was a bug-infested mattress that he'd found in a Dumpster. He could barely afford to eat, much less buy furniture. But Dwayne had a dream. He'd show them what Dwayne Johnson could do on the football field. He had greatness in him, coursing through his genes. Dwayne knew that some way, somehow, he'd make his mark.

Dwayne was right, of course. Only he was wrong about one thing: It wasn't going to be in football. He just didn't know it then — so he pressed on.

How low did Dwayne go? Pretty low. So low, in fact, that his spirit was nearly broken. His football career was a bust. He'd missed too much time on the field. Plus, the CFL had a lot of politics, too. Each team could only have a limited number of non-Canadians on the roster. It was the rule. The Canadian fans wanted to see at least *some* Canadian football players. It didn't help Dwayne Johnson's career any. He was cut from the team in October 1995.

Dwayne returned home to Dany and talked it over. He'd made a decision. He told her that he wanted to become a professional wrestler. But first, he needed Dany's approval. He loved her and he needed her support. Without it, Dwayne could not — would not — travel the long, hard road ahead. That night, after all the discussion, the tears and emotion, Dany pledged her support.

When you want to become a doctor, you go to medical college. A lawyer? You get yourself into law school. But what if, like Dwayne Johnson, you wanted to become a professional wrestler? Well, pack your bags. It's time for wrestling school. Fortunately, Dwayne had a few connections in the business.

He called Rocky Johnson.

CHAPTER 9
Selling the Show

You know when a wrestler is tangled up like a pretzel, and he's howling in pain, screaming, and banging the mat, just *dying* out there? Well, that's called "selling." And it means exactly what it sounds like. He's acting, putting on a show, working hard to convince the fans that he's genuinely in pain. Because even though we know, *we know*, it's not real, some small part of us wants to believe. The fans want the illusion.

Fans appreciate the drama and the magic. It may be done with mirrors, or scripts, but who really cares? It's still great entertainment. And it's accomplished by uniquely powerful men with an uncommon blend of superior athleticism, old-fashioned ruggedness, and a showman's gift for performing.

When we sit in a movie theater, we *want* to be taken away by a great story. We want to believe. And if the actor sells it well enough, really *sells* it, we will believe. If only for a moment.

It *feels* real. That's selling.

As The Rock wrote in his autobiography, *The Rock Says . . .* , "This business is a work, which is another way of saying that the results are predetermined, and we all know it. Winning isn't the point — doing your job and doing it well is all that matters."

GETTING POP

The Rock is known for getting "tremendous pop" from an audience. What's pop? It's a sudden burst of applause from the crowd. A giant, collective, "WOW!" For a professional entertainer like The Rock, getting good pop is what it's all about.

CHAPTER 10
Wrestling School

Dwayne was excited. Sure, he had only seven dollars to his name. And he'd been bitterly disappointed in Canada. But a bright new dream swelled his heart.

It felt so right. Just like that first time he met Dany. Dwayne was convinced, down to the bone. His destiny was as a wrestler. Looking back on his life, his heritage, it only made sense.

Rocky Johnson oversaw his son's education in the ring, setting him up with various trainers. Dwayne soon settled into a grueling routine of training, lifting, studying, and training some more. In between, he slept, ate, and worked a day job as a personal trainer. Dwayne was obsessed, completely dedicated to becoming a professional wrestler.

When he gained confidence in his abilities, Dwayne made a call to an old family friend. Pat Patterson was a former wrestler who'd long ago grappled against Dwayne's grandfather, the High Chief. Patterson worked for the WWF, the World Wrestling Federation. He was an influential man in the business.

Patterson agreed to watch Dwayne work out. He came away impressed; Dwayne was raw, but he had natural instincts. Plus, he was good-looking young man, and that never hurt.

The kid had potential.

Patterson called the owner of the WWF, Vince McMahon, a remarkable businessman capable of making and breaking careers with a single decision. Patterson told Dwayne to fly to Corpus Christi, Texas, for a match. Vince McMahon would attend. He wanted to see Dwayne for himself.

It was a huge moment in Dwayne's life. A crossroads. He was determined to make the most of it. His opponent in his first professional match, in front of 15,000 fans, was to be Steve Lombardi, who wrestled under the name the Brooklyn Brawler.

Steve Lombardi couldn't have been nicer. He welcomed Dwayne with a handshake and a smile. The plan was for Steve to lose the match — *to*

RING LINGO

The Lock-Up: When two wrestlers, after sizing each other up, first join in a clench. *Shoot Off:* To throw someone against the ropes. *Spot:* Any specific wrestling move is called a spot. *Running Spots:* A sequence of moves. *Getting Potatoed:* Getting hit too hard in the ring, usually because your opponent is "too stiff." *Put Him Over:* Let your opponent win.

put Dwayne over, as they say — and Steve had no problem with that. He was a real pro who understood the business. Over lunch, they came up with a decent routine.

The match went perfectly as planned. Dwayne Johnson (he hadn't yet come up with a ring name) defeated the mighty Brooklyn Brawler — pinned him right there in the middle of the ring. Vince McMahon came away impressed — sort of. Dwayne was offered a job to wrestle out of Memphis for the United States Wrestling Alliance. The USWA had ties to the WWF, and Vince sent many beginning wrestlers to Memphis to improve their skills. In Vince's eyes, Dwayne was not yet ready for prime time. The message was clear: Dwayne would have to hone his act out of the WWF's bright spotlight. Build his abilities.

Develop his character. Work like a dog. In other words, *Don't call us, we'll call you.*

That was all good with Dwayne Johnson. Hard work didn't scare him. But most important, Dwayne knew that his life was on the right path. What's more, Dwayne came up with what he considered to be a pretty cool-sounding ring name. He'd wrestle as — hold on to your sick bags, ladies and gentlemen — Flex Kavana!

CHAPTER 11
The Survivor

Few wrestlers, if any, had a WWF debut like Dwayne Johnson. Sure, he'd worked hard for this moment. He'd trained hard in Memphis for nearly five months, refining his moves, becoming more comfortable with his ring persona. Dwayne had put in his time. He felt ready for the big leagues.

But was he ready *for this*?

The place was Madison Square Garden, one of the most celebrated arenas in the world. It was November 16, 1996. The event was the Survivor Series. Eight men, loosely assembled in two teams, would enter the ring. Elimination was by pin only — one, two, three, you're history. At the end, one wrestler would survive. The winner.

It was Marc Mero, Barry Windham, Jake Roberts,

38

The Rock was born to wrestle. His dad did — as well as his Native American grandfather.

The Rock socks it to all contenders!

"Do you smell what The Rock is cooking?"
That's one of his catchphrases. How many
more do you know?

When he was known as Rocky Maivia,
he took on Cactus Jack, now known as Mankind.
Guess who won?

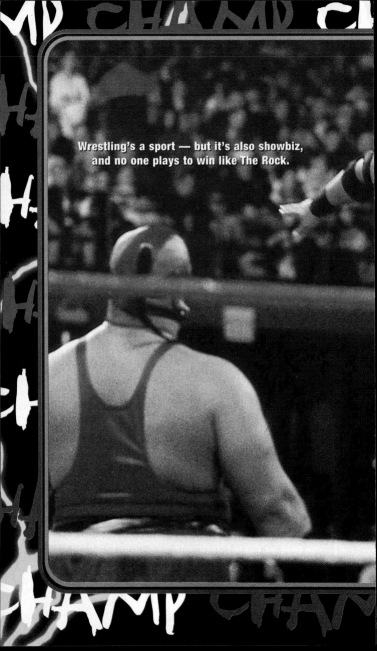

Wrestling's a sport — but it's also showbiz, and no one plays to win like The Rock.

The Rock is a well-oiled machine.

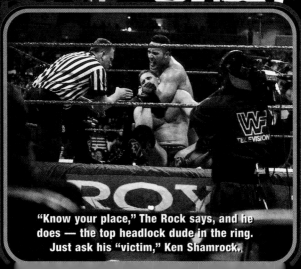

"Know your place," The Rock says, and he does — the top headlock dude in the ring. Just ask his "victim," Ken Shamrock.

He's the champ, so bring on the chumps!

Believe it or not, there is a quiet,
thoughtful side to the man. And a soft side.
He dedicated his book to his mom.

Call him what you will: King of the Ring,
The People's Champion — the Rock is a superstar.
He's earned it all.

and Dwayne (wrestling under the name Rocky Maivia — more on that, later) battling against Goldust, Hunter Hearst Helmsley, Jerry Lawler, and Crush. A solid group of wrestlers. Not federation superstars, but several were clearly on their way to bigger, better things.

By midday, the wrestlers still didn't know what the outcome would be. Then Gerry Brisco, a WWF official, gave them the news. Dwayne had been selected to win the match.

No, Dwayne didn't fall off his chair in a dead faint. But it was close. After all, he was an unknown, making his professional debut. It was truly shocking to be presented with such a huge opportunity this soon in his career. Dwayne promised to make the most of it. Inwardly, his heart soared. Dwayne recognized that it was a huge statement from the WWF: They saw a future in Dwayne Johnson.

By that time, mercifully, the stage name Flex Kavana had been dropped, kicked around, and buried. Vince McMahon and the WWF officials were well aware that Dwayne was the first WWF wrestler whose father *and* grandfather had wrestled for the company. That made Dwayne a third-generation wrestler — and they wanted a name to reflect that fact. So they proposed *Rocky Maivia*, combining

Dwayne's father's first name with his famous grand-father's last name.

Dwayne thought it over. He wasn't so sure. But, well, okay, why not? It beat Flex Kavana any day of the week. During introductions, the crowd didn't pay much attention to Rocky Maivia. He was a smiling rookie, an unknown, and they didn't particularly care. But half an hour later, when he pinned Goldust, Rocky Maivia was the last man standing. Rocky looked out into the crowd, proud and triumphant.

There was a new man in town.

CHAPTER 12
Heels and Baby Faces

Traditionally, there are two kinds of wrestlers. The good guys, and the bad guys. The good guys are fair and honest, proud and brave. In the business, they are called *baby faces*. The Rock's father, for example, fought throughout his career as a baby face.

The bad guys are a different kind of wrestler. The bad guys, known as *heels*, are bad to the bone. They're rude, egotistical, and arrogant. They cheat, spit, and *say* outrageous things. Then they *do* far worse. The reason for this? When fans see a match, they like to do two things: 1) They like to cheer; and 2) They like to boo. It's that simple. In the perfect match, you need a heel and you need a baby face. You need a hero and you need a villain.

And that's the way it's been for a long, long time.

Dwayne started out as a baby face. It just seemed right at the time. He was supposed to portray an all-around good guy. Smile a lot. Be sweet. Happy. The kind of guy you'd invite home to meet the folks. A guy who'd be kind to small animals, help old people across the street, brush his teeth twice before going to bed. A boy scout in wrestling tights.

Well, maybe that hit too close to home. Because Dwayne Johnson was, authentically, a good guy. So maybe, as Rocky Maivia, he smiled *too much*. Maybe he looked too perfect, with that striking blend of African-American and Samoan blood. Maybe too nice. Too straight.

Too . . . *dull*.

Times had changed. There had been a tidal shift among fans — and Dwayne found himself portraying an old-fashioned baby face when the crowd craved attitude, rebellion, individuality, and aggressiveness. They liked their wrestlers with an *edge*.

An early sign of the fans' discontent with Rocky Maivia came in early 1997, when Hunter Hearst Helmsley dropped the Intercontinental Championship belt to Rocky. The Intercontinental title was a valued prize, second only to the World Wrestling Federation Championship.

The match represented a great victory for Rocky.

A significant step up the ladder. But for the fans, it was a shocking turn of events. Rocky was too young to win a title. In their eyes, he hadn't *earned* it yet. Rocky Maivia, after all, was only twenty-four years old. The youngest Intercontinental Champion ever.

And he was dull.

That night, a smattering of boos came from the Lowell, Massachusetts, crowd. Not a downpour of disgust, just a few jeers, some scattered catcalls. The rest of the crowd remained silent. It wasn't outrage, exactly; but few in attendance were pleased.

It was a classic example of how, at the end of the day, the fans have a lot more power than they realize. Because all anybody in the WWF really wants to do is please the fans — and keep 'em coming back for more. More shirts, more glossy programs, more pay-per-views. When the fans speak, the WWF listens.

And, for better or worse, the fans were talking about Rocky Maivia.

CHAPTER 13
Trouble Cooking

The fans in Chicago, Illinois, spoke even louder at WrestleMania XIII. More and more, the paying customer seemed drawn to the heels — or the bad guys. Times were changing. Wrestling needed to change with it.

Strangely, the thick line between heel and baby face began to blur. Today, the hero often acts like a heel. There aren't too many classic baby faces in the business anymore. Even the biggest baby face of professional wrestling, Hulk Hogan, has taken a walk on the dark side.

Of course, it's not all clear-cut. Public reaction shifts on a weekly basis. Rocky Maivia got caught in the middle. And his career was about to be turned upside down.

WrestleMania is the single most popular event in wrestling. It's a huge moneymaker for the WWF. It's their pay-per-view event of the year. To participate in it is an honor. A chance to shine before millions . . . *and millions*.

Rocky was scheduled to defend the Intercontinental belt against the Sultan, a heel from parts unknown in the Middle East. To make him even more loathsome to the fans, Sultan was managed by the dreaded Iron Sheik, a classic heel.

The announcer spoke into the microphone: "*Ladies and gentlemen, from Miami, Florida, weighing 275 pounds, Rocky Maivia!*"

At first, it was just a smattering of boos. Rocky walked down the ramp. The boos grew louder. Rocky headed toward the ring. More boos, then a light chant echoed through the rafters that let everyone know how they felt about Rocky: "Rocky stinks! Rocky stinks!" (Actually, what they really said was a little bit worse, but the sentiment is the same.)

Rocky stepped into the ring and faced the crowd. Louder and louder, more and more voices joined the chorus.

Somewhere beneath the tough exterior of Rocky Maivia, another man heard the jeering with shock and disappointment. Dwayne Johnson was confused. *"Wait a minute . . . I'm the good guy!* That was the first thought that went through my mind," Dwayne recalled in his autobiography *The Rock Says . . .* "Somewhere along the line, something had gone terribly wrong. I had put in so much work, and I had done exactly what I was told to do. I had embraced a character who was supposed to be a classic baby face, and for some reason that character was now reviled. It made no sense."

Rocky went on to defeat the Sultan in a decent, crowd-pleasing bout, retaining the Intercontinental Championship. To add to the fans' home-viewing pleasure, Rocky Johnson, former champion, joined the fray, helping to stave off an attack on his son from the Iron Sheik.

Yes, Rocky had the belt.

But to the people, he was no champion.

CHAPTER 14
Die, Rocky, Die

In 1996, Rocky Maivia was ranked #167 in the world. By the end of 1997, he'd climbed to a ranking of #103.

It was a struggle every step of the way. In the ring, there were nights when Rocky, with his inexperience, was eaten alive by WWF veterans. The fans were even rougher. After WrestleMania XIII, the anti-Rocky feeling continued to swell. It was "Rocky Stinks!" at every stop on the tour. To make things perfectly clear, just to avoid any misunderstanding whatsoever, several fans held up signs that spelled it out:

"D-I-E, R-O-C-K-Y, D-I-E!"

At first, Rocky smiled through it all. Pretended not to hear the jeers. But after a while, Rocky

Maivia stopped smiling. Part of that was by design, a decision to toughen up his character. Part of it was a genuine, honest reaction. Meanwhile, Rocky continued to work — long and hard — on his fighting ability. He didn't give up. He kept learning the craft, the art of the ring. He was becoming a vastly improved wrestler.

Not long after WrestleMania XIII, Rocky injured his knee. The knee required rest. So he took eight weeks off.

It gave Dwayne a chance to think. And this is how he figured it. If the fans were going to boo, well then, why not *give* them something to boo about? Dwayne knew that pure wrestling ability, no matter how spectacular, was only one ingredient in the making of a successful wrestler. There's a long list of athletes with solid technical ability who never managed to capture the imagination of the fans. The fans enjoy the soap opera. The character. All that crazy stuff outside the ring. Dwayne knew that. He realized it was time to make some changes.

He talked it over with his bosses in the WWF. Happily, everyone agreed. After all, the fans had spoken. It was time to find a style to match his physique. Time to let all the bottled up aggression, all the simmering ambition, come pouring forth. More than that. It was time to *exaggerate* everything. The ego, the I'm-all-that attitude, the vanity. Just blow it all up larger than life.

In professional wrestling, as in real life, you are judged by the company you keep. So Rocky Maivia decided to make a few, nasty friends. He joined an angry faction of WWF rebels called the Nation of Domination, lead by a heel named Farooq (played by Ron Simmons). One night, to the shock of those in attendance, Rocky Maivia helped Farooq out in a tussle he was having with a baby face named Chainz. In a stunning maneuver — later dubbed "The Rock Bottom"— Rocky drove Chainz practically through the mat, saving Farooq from sure defeat.

The crowd angrily booed the WWF's latest heel.

And deep in his heart, Dwayne Johnson was happy. He was finally giving a great performance, inside the ring *and* out. A few nights later, on national television, Rocky grabbed a microphone and addressed the hostile crowd. He glared with feigned anger. "That's the response I get from you people?" he snarled. "After giving my blood, my sweat, and my tears? For months and months? Signs that say '*Die, Rocky, Die*'?"

THE PEOPLE'S EYEBROW

Outside of Mr. Spock from the original *Star Trek* series, The Rock features the most incredible eyebrow to hit national television. He cocks his head, attitude in his eye, and liftoff — *The People's Eyebrow*. For Dwayne, it was just a little trick he could do to get a laugh from friends. He'd walk down the corridors of Freedom High, see a group of pals, lift an eyebrow, and it would all be good. Little did he realize that his little trick would one day be featured on the cover of *Newsweek* magazine.

The crowd was silenced.

This was something new. Before their eyes, Rocky Maivia was changing. He had an edge. From now on, he demanded — and commanded — respect.

CHAPTER 15
Birth of The Rock

Every superhero has it. That day of transformation, when everything changes. *Everything*.

Take Peter Parker for instance. We all know the story (at least all of us intellectuals who read comic books). Pale, skinny Peter Parker — the type of guy whom The Rock would call a *jabroni* — went off to a science lab instead of a beach party. He was eager to witness an experiment with radioactivity. It was an ordinary day in every way, except for one thing. He was bitten by a radioactive spider.

From that moment forward, Peter Parker became Spider-Man. No longer the geek.

No longer a jabroni.

Rocky Maivia has a similar transformation. For on

a December night in 1997, Rocky Maivia faded into the mist, into the background.

The scene was set. Stone Cold Steve Austin was the Intercontinental titleholder. Austin's favorite way of ending an interview was by stating, "And that's the bottom line —'cause Stone Cold said so!" In the middle of the ring, Rocky stepped up and challenged Steve Austin to a title match. He glared at Austin and threatened: "And if you accept my challenge, then *your* bottom line will say: *Stone Cold has-been. Compliments of . . . The Rock!*"

Good-bye Rocky Maivia.

For on that day, The Rock was born.

The happy-go-lucky baby face was gone. The scowling, eyebrow-raising, proud master of the put-down took over. The Rock was serving notice to the other competitors of the WWF.

Later that same month, Austin handed the Intercontinental title over to The Rock. Literally *handed* it over. Austin had outgrown the IC title and was now set on becoming the WWF world champion. He served the Rock the IC title on a sliver platter — and then performed his finisher, the Stone-Cold Stunner, on the new IC champion!

The Rock's character continued to evolve. He was getting tougher, harder, meaner — and more humorous. Each time he got the opportunity, The Rock delighted fans with his skills on the microphone. He may not have been the nice guy Rocky Maivia was, but The Rock was a lot more entertaining.

In spring of 1998, Intercontinental titleholder The Rock squared off against challenger Ken Shamrock at WrestleMania XIV. The bout was not a pretty sight. As the Rock entered the ring, the crowd responded by raining boos down on The Rock's head.

Ken Shamrock had the body of someone who spent a lot of time flexing in front of the mirror. Shamrock was a former Ultimate Fighting Championship winner. He was billed as "the world's most dangerous man." He was obviously the crowd favorite.

Shamrock had a weakness, however: his legendary temper. Once he snapped, there was no telling what he'd do. Suddenly a crazed look would come over him; he'd stare blindly with vacant eyes. The lights were on, but Ken Shamrock wasn't home.

Shamrock dominated the match, setting the pace with a flurry of offensive rallies. The Rock hung tough and took his beating. At one point, Shamrock brought a chair into the ring. The Rock grabbed ahold of it, smashing it on Shamrock's thick skull.

By some miracle, Shamrock was able to kick out of The Rock's pin attempt.

Once again, Shamrock gained the upper hand. Suddenly, he had The Rock down, and applied an anklelock. The anklelock is a submission hold. The idea is to hold an opponent still while causing so much suffering, such searing torture, that your opponent "taps out," or surrenders the match.

Which is exactly what The Rock did.

Shamrock was the winner. The new Intercontinental Champion. But wait . . .

Even though The Rock had tapped out, Shamrock refused to release the hold. The Rock cried out in agony. Four referees and two WWF officials, dressed in business suits, entered the ring. But Shamrock had snapped! One by one, he drove each referee to the mat with a suplex. Meanwhile, a destroyed Rock was being wheeled toward the exit on a stretcher.

Hold on. There was an announcement. The judge had reversed the decision! Shamrock was automatically disqualified for not releasing the submission hold. The Rock retained the Intercontinental title.

Shamrock went berserk! He raced after The Rock, spilling him off the stretcher onto the concrete floor. Shamrock laid such a nasty beating on The Rock that he may have fondly recalled sixteen-year-old Billy and a long-ago day in junior high. Finally, Shamrock grabbed the belt. He held it high, threw it down in disgust, and stormed off. Beaten and bloodied, an absolute wreck, The Rock retained his Intercontinental title.

While fights and storylines like this one *are* carefully choreographed, sometimes accidents do happen, and as you'll see in the next chapter, injuries — very real ones — do occur.

CHAPTER 16
All Too Real

Although professional wrestling is a *work*, that doesn't mean it's fake. There remain a lot of things about professional wrestling that are very, very real.

And dangerous. The wrestler Mick Foley (a.k.a. Mankind, Dude Love, and Cactus Jack), for example, has suffered a staggering number of serious ring-related injuries, including: broken cheekbone, second-degree burns, broken wrist, torn abdominal, bruised kidney, broken jaw, eight concussions, fractured left shoulder, five broken ribs . . . and, well, you should get the idea. Don't tell Mick Foley it's not real.

On October 5, 1999, Darren Drosdov was left paralyzed after performing a standard wrestling move. In the midst of a match against D-Lo Brown at the Nassau Coliseum in Uniondale, New York, Drosdov landed awkwardly. The match was stopped immediately as emergency crews rushed to Drosdov's fallen body. Later in the hospital, two disks were removed from his spine. Surgeons used a piece of his pelvis to replace the disks. A metal plate and screws stabilized his neck. For Drosdov, there's still hope. Doctors feel he may walk again.

But when counting ring tragedies — when the show becomes frighteningly real — one only needs to remember the death of Owen Hart. For on May 23, 1999, in Kansas City, Missouri, Hart attempted a sensational descent into the ring for his match against The Godfather. Owen Hart, younger brother of Bret "The Hitman" Hart, dangled from a cable ninety feet in the air and began his stylish entrance.

Some in the crowd gasped with delight. Then, as Hart was being lowered into the ring, his cable accidentally released. He crashed to the turnbuckle below, dying almost immediately. For a few moments, the crowd stood confused, uncertain. Was this part of the show? Just an incredible stunt? Was it real?

Yes, tragically, all too real.

The Rock was there that day, backstage, waiting for his turn in the ring. He was going over the routine for that night's match against Triple H and Chyna. Know this: Owen Hart was The Rock's — no, *Dwayne's* — good friend. Hart was a professional, a devoted family man, and a big practical joker. At first, The Rock didn't know just what to think. Was this another one of Owen's insane jokes?

Was it a work?

Minutes before he was to enter the ring, The Rock learned that Owen had died. The Rock was numb, in shock. Still, the arena was filled with fans. It was a pay-per-view show, with half a million home viewers glued to their television sets. The fans had paid good money. And they wanted a good show in return.

The company of wrestlers, a *family*, really, quickly got together and made a decision. The show would go on. Somehow The Rock got through it. To him, it felt like the right thing to do. He felt Owen would have wanted it that way. The Rock understood that Owen Hart came from a family steeped in the wrestling tradition. Everyone in the business re-spected the Harts. They were the real deal. And Owen Hart knew as well as anyone that the show must, *it must*, go on.

And it did.

CHAPTER 17
Talking the Talk

The Rock continued earning attention and respect throughout 1998. In SummerSlam '98, he lost a horrific ladder match to Triple H and Chyna. A ladder match is considered one of the most dangerous matches in wrestling. A title belt is suspended above the ring. A ladder is brought to ringside. The object is to be the first man to climb the ladder and grab the belt. However, the ladder can be used as a weapon during the match.

Even in defeat, The Rock showed genuine toughness. The fans saw that he'd become a more skilled wrestler. Plus, they now knew they could count on The Rock to entertain them. He was *dependable*. One way or the other, win or lose, it was always fun when The Rock was in the house.

When opportunity knocked, The Rock was primed and ready to unleash perhaps his greatest gift: His mouth. That's how he became The People's Champion. By *telling* them he was. Like a king, the self-styled Great One proclaimed it. But you know what? The people didn't disagree.

Despite his incredible athleticism, his staggering physical gifts, The Rock became famous because of his mouth. Put a microphone before his face, and he lit up like a firecracker.

The Rock lingo is priceless. *Jabroni. Know your role. It doesn't matter what your name is. Lay the smack down. Shut your mouth. Know your role.*

Plus, he gave his moves exciting names: *The Rock Bottom. The People's Elbow. The Samoan Drop.*

And, of course, there is his most famous expression of all: "*If you SMELL what The Rock is cooking.*"

Mere hours after hearing a new catchphrase from the Rock, fans imitate it whole-heartedly. Nowadays, The Rock can hardly finish a sentence without twenty thousand screaming men and women joining in.

The Rock: "If you smelllll . . ."

The crowd: ". . . WHAT THE ROCK IS COOKING!"

LAYING THE SMACK DOWN

February 14, 1999, Memphis, Tennessee, birthplace of Elvis Presley. In the middle of a classic brawl, The Rock stood over Mankind's prone body. He grabbed a microphone, sneered his lip like Elvis, and began to sing. *"Well, since Rock's baby left him, he's found a new place to dwell. It's down at the end of Jabroni Drive at ... Smack Down Hotel!"* The phrase became a classic, and a website and television commercial are dedicated to the imaginary Smack Down Hotel.

The Rock takes that part of the business seriously. He's constantly jotting down ideas on napkins, scraps of paper, whatever's around. Cutting promos is the most important part of a wrestler's job. They have a few moments to prerecord a message to their opponent that is played right before the match. The Rock doesn't write out each promo word for word, but he does make outlines. When it's time to talk, The Rock knows where he's going.

In a 2000 interview with Tony Morrow of Scrips Howard News Service, Dwayne explained it this way. "The Rock is still Dwayne Johnson, but Dwayne Johnson with the volume turned up to its highest level, magnified one hundred thousand times."

By the end of 1998, The Rock was ranked #11 in all of professional wrestling. Something else was happening as well. People were beginning to *cheer* The Rock. Suddenly they couldn't get enough of The Rock. Good guy, heel, who cares? He simply had too much, well, *Rockness*, to resist.

And he was ready launch his best year ever. Because 1999 was going to be . . . The Year of The Rock.

CHAPTER 18
Mankind

No book on The Rock would be complete without giving credit to Mankind, for his part in their spectacular rivalry. Their series of battles and promos are among the most entertaining in recent history, raising both of their profiles (and merchandising sales!) into the upper decks, through the roof, and into orbit. In 1999, The Rock and Mankind staged some of the most compelling, extraordinary ring wars that have been seen in the WWF since, well, never.

Mankind, the character, came from the highly creative brain of longtime professional wrestler, Mick Foley. Of course, he got a little guidance along the way from WWF mastermind, Vince McMahon.

Mick Foley was a wrestler's wrestler, long admired by many in the wrestling business. He made his professional debut in June 1983. He was a veteran of countless matches. He knew every inch of the ring. He'd seen it all and done it all — wrestled in exploding rings, in cage matches, boiler rooms, Dumpster matches, ladder matches, and more. In fact, it's quite possible that Foley had fought in every conceivable specialty match known to wrestling. He'd been involved in some of the most famous battles ever held, including the 1998 Hell in a Cell match against The Undertaker. It was a brutal cage match that sent Foley to the hospital.

Foley had performed under two names before the "birth" of Mankind. He'd worked as psychotic Cactus Jack and as the far-out and freaky Dude Love (with his James Brown-styled catch phrase, "*Owww. Have mercy.*"). But the character of Mankind — life's lovable loser in a leather mask and loopy, lopsided smile — well, that was pure brilliance. Still, it took a grappler with Foley's ring experience to pull it off.

To go along with the character of Mankind, Foley knew he needed a new finishing move. It's critically important for wrestlers to offer the fans something unique — a signature move that sets them apart. The Rock had "The Rock Bottom" and "The Peo-

THE ROCK BOTTOM

The Rock's signature move, the devastating "Rock Bottom," requires a furious thrust of the right arm and lower body — as he lifts his opponent into the air and hurls him onto the mat. It takes serious precision and strength. Take that, jabroni!

ple's Elbow." Triple H had "The Pedigree." Goldberg had the Jackhammer." Steve Austin had, as most everyone knew, the famous "Stone Cold Stunner."

Foley knew he needed something strange. Something sinister. Something a little bit sick. Something like . . . *the mandible claw*. The science behind the move was simple enough. You pressed down beneath your opponent's tongue with two middle fingers, putting pressure on the nerves. At the same time, you pressed up with the thumb under the chin. Supposedly, this would paralyze the opponent, allowing for an easy pin.

Mick Foley had his finishing move.

But Mick Foley was about to give his character one last, very interesting *twist*.

In a truly inspired WWF storyline, it was decided that Mankind would become hopelessly devoted to Vince McMahon, to the point of even calling him . . . DAD. Of course, even though McMahon played a classic corporate heel, hated by nearly everyone in the business, the last person he wanted to have actually *like* him was the seemingly deranged Mankind.

McMahon, as the promos soon showed, wanted *nothing* to do with Mankind's endless (and pathetic) shows of friendship. It was classic WWF soap opera, played with expert comic timing by Foley and McMahon.

In one famous setup, Vince was taken to the hospital with a hurt ankle. The idea for the skit was that Mankind would visit Vince, just to cheer him up. Again, outside of archrival Steve Austin, Mankind was the last person Vince McMahon wanted to see.

Foley's imagination caught fire. He thought long and hard about the skit, and showed up at "the hospital" prepared with an armload of goofy gifts: helium balloons, a box of half-eaten chocolates (he'd gotten hungry, he sheepishly explained), and an extra special surprise.

At one point, Mankind slid under McMahon's bed, slipped an old sweat sock on his hand, and began to speak in the high-pitched squeak of the world's lamest ventriloquist: *"Hi, I'm Mr. Socko, and I've come to save the day. I hear you have a boo-boo, and Mr. Socko is going to kiss it and make it feel better."*

"No, NO!" screamed Vince McMahon, fearful and disgusted. "Leave! Leave! NOW!"

It was, no doubt, one of the funniest moments in WWF television history. The very next night, the arena was jammed with fans carrying signs about Mr. Socko. Again, the fans had spoken. From that day on, Mr. Socko would be the one applying the mandible claw.

So this was the jabroni that The Rock — the coolest cat on the planet — had to fight to win the greatest prize in professional wrestling: The World Wrestling Federation Championship.

Does it get any better than that?

CHAPTER 19
A Heel of a Thing to Do

Professional wrestling is famous for its betrayals. Brothers turn against brothers, baby faces turn heel, honor and loyalty are tossed out of the window. It happens often, usually before a packed crowd. Usually with a lot of careful planning by the staff writers at the WWF.

The Rock/Mankind rivalry first heated up in late 1998, in a fourteen-man Survivor Series that was set to determine the WWF Championship. This was a big one. At the time, Mankind believed that Vince McMahon was his *friend*. Which is like a mouse trusting a back alley tomcat.

The series involved the biggest names in the WWF. To reach the final, Mankind had to eliminate Duane Gill, Al Snow, and Steve Austin (who lost under suspicious circumstances involving match referee Shane McMahon, son of Vince). The Rock put the hurt on Big Bossman, Ken Shamrock, and The Undertaker. The final match was set. Mankind, a scraggy-haired, shuffling, shambling mess of a man . . . against his polar opposite, The Rock.

Under normal circumstances, wrestlers will discuss a match beforehand. Go over a few moves, come up with a general routine. But not this time. The Rock and Mankind had to wing it. Mick Foley admitted in his book, *Have a Nice Day*: "I really had no clue what I was going to do in this huge main event. I was physically exhausted and mentally drained. For a wrestler with only two years of experience, The Rock had incredible poise in the ring, but he too looked worn and confused. We locked up, *and I drew a blank*."

Gradually, thanks to the professionalism of the athletes involved, the match built momentum. At one point, after falling from the turnbuckle onto a table, Mankind dislocated a kneecap and tore a ligament. Did Mick Foley quit? Not on your life, brother. Out came Mr. Socko into Rock's mouth. The Rock kicked out of the mandible claw. He lowered the boom on Mankind by delivering The People's Elbow. Mankind kicked out. The battle raged on as the crowd, pumped to a frenzy, stood and screamed.

The Rock had Mankind in trouble again. He applied the Sharpshooter, locking Mankind's legs and lower back in an excruciating hold. *Ding, ding, ding!* The match was over. The Rock was declared the winner — thanks to Vince McMahon and a very, very fast bell. McMahon had called for the bell, even though Mankind had not given up in the submission hold.

Mankind looked up in disbelief as Vince McMahon, *his friend*, entered the ring. McMahon, all smiles, handed The Rock the belt. The two men shook hands. And hugged. Immediately, everyone realized that The Rock had been in cahoots with that hated corporate creep all along. The crowd voiced their disapproval.

In one instant, The Rock had turned mega-heel before their eyes. To make matters worse, the sympathy for the hurt, bewildered Mankind ("I thought you were my friend," he whined) was enormous. The Rock declared himself Corporate Champion. And Mankind vowed revenge.

The stage was set for a thrilling series of matches in which Mankind and The Rock traded the belt four times. A few highlights:

In one match, billed as "Halftime Heat" because it took place during halftime of the Super Bowl, the two men fought inside an empty arena. When the fight spilled over to the arena's backrooms, Mankind won the match in a most unusual way. He pinned the Rock using a forklift, dropping a wooden pallet on his chest!

There was an "I Quit" match at The Royal Rumble, when The Rock forced Mankind to scream, "I quit! I quit!" But could that be possible? From Mankind, a brawler who seemed to actually *enjoy* pain? As it turned out, the answer was no. A faked tape was played into a microphone, making it *seem* like Mankind had quit. Once again, he was robbed of the title.

Don't feel too bad for Mankind, though. He regained the title in late January, with the help of Steve Austin, a folding chair, and The Rock's battered skull. On February 14, 1999, on the anniversary of the St. Valentine's Day Massacre, The Rock and Mankind entered a Last-Man-Standing Match. This amazing match swung back and forth, thrilling the crowd, and ended when both wrestlers smashed each other's head with metal chairs . . . *simultaneously*! Both were disqualified when neither one could get up off the canvas.

The next night, in Birmingham, Alabama, The Rock regained the belt for the third time.

Next up: WrestleMania XV, for The Rock's greatest night in his professional career (so far). A title match against Stone Cold Steve Austin, with millions . . . *and millions* . . . watching.

CHAPTER 20
Greatness

Forgive Dwayne Johnson if, before stepping out into the frenzied mob at WrestleMania XV — before becoming The Rock once more — he takes a moment to let it all sink in.

He'd come so far to get to this point. For here he stood, at the apex of a dream, about to perform in the title match in the biggest wrestling event in history. The WWF's two top superstars: Stone Cold Steve Austin versus The Rock. For the belt.

Dwayne thought of his beloved grandfather, who had since passed away, and wished he could share in this moment with Dwayne. He thought of Dany, who'd stood by him through thick and thin. His grandmother, Leah Maivia. His parents, Rocky and Ata. And all those people who helped him along the way. And forgive him, please, for remembering every person who ever doubted him, ever questioned his ability, and ever refused to believe in Dwayne Johnson. Because look at him now. The Rock was the biggest draw in the most watched wrestling event . . . *ever held.*

Dwayne got the signal, a few last pats on the back, calls of "good luck" and "put on a great show." The music blasted out of the speakers, rattling the walls of the First Union Center.

Like so many times before, Dwayne Johnson faded into the background. Because now, holding the World Wrestling Federation belt high in the air, stepped forth . . . The Rock.

And the place . . . went . . . nuts.

The match had been carefully planned. Dwayne and Austin had gone over the routine, time and again. They discussed it over meals, in the hallways, in dressing rooms. They went over different spots, tossing ideas back and forth. Until, finally, it was fully choreographed. Both men were determined to put on a brawl no one would soon forget.

And they did just that.

The match had it all. The People's Elbow. The Rock Bottom. Three different referees knocked out and disabled. Backflips and boots to the midsection and last-second kickouts and — can you believe this? — Mankind in a referee's shirt. Smashed chairs and two Stone Cold Stunners. For thirty high-intensity minutes, before a thrilled crowd of 21,000 screaming fans, the gladiators went at it tooth and nail, pouring every last ounce of energy into one of the greatest matches ever.

Finally, it happened. One, two, three, pin.

The Rock dropped the belt to Stone Cold Steve Austin.

Backstage, drenched with sweat, exhausted yet elated, Dwayne Johnson said a silent prayer, thanking God for allowing it all to happen. The greatest night in his professional career. A few moments later Steve Austin entered the room. Steve was more than a great wrestler. Much more. He was Dwayne's friend. The two stood in the center of the room and embraced.

High Chief Peter Maivia would have been proud.

CHAPTER 21
The Rock and Sock Combination

As the Corporate Champion, Rock was a super heel. But in the weeks after Wrestlemania XV, he fell out of favor with Vince McMahon. However, that didn't hurt his career any. He was still The People's Champion, and he was about to become more popular than ever — thanks to an unlikely partner.

It began with a televised match on Raw, when The Rock was in trouble against two opponents.

Out of nowhere, the wrestler Mankind raced to his rescue. Afterwards, Mankind made an offer to The Rock: "You know what I can do in the ring, and

I know what you can do. I think we'd make a good team."

Suddenly, The Rock was Mankind's new best friend. In one inspired bit (and ratings bonanza), Mankind decided to show his friendship by putting on a "This Is Your Life" segment in honor of The Rock.

For twenty minutes the skit rolled along with The Rock playing off Mankind beautifully — frowning, grumpy, obviously irritated. Meanwhile, oblivious, Mankind prattled on. The Rock grew increasingly disgusted, the humor bubbling forth between the two comic performers. Finally, Mankind presented a gift of Mr. Rocko — a sock with The Rock's face painted on it!

The Rock was less than thrilled with Mankind's attention. He got irritated when Mankind began to copy The Rock's expressions. When The Rock talked about his "millions . . . and millions" of fans, Mankind felt a need to mention his "dozens . . . and dozens."

Still, in the ring, they were an undeniable force. They first captured the WWF World-Tag-Team Championship in August 1999, when they combined to give The Big Show "The People's Elbow" simultaneously! They lost and won the belt two more times, setting up one last, classic bit of comedy.

To say that Mankind was getting on The Rock's nerves was an understatement. One day, Mankind made a point of giving The Rock an inscribed copy of *Have a Nice Day*. The Rock was not what you'd call thrilled about it. Later on, wrestler Al Snow found that same, inscribed book in a garbage can! Did The Rock throw Mick Foley's life story into a foul, smelly, garbage can? (*The plot thickened*: Some contended that the book was planted by Snow himself, who then went on to become Mankind's tag-team partner.)

Mankind was shattered. Tears in his eyes, he confronted The Rock in the locker room. He said he never, ever wanted anything to do with The Rock again. That was cool with The Rock. Except for one small problem. They were supposed to defend the belt that night against the Holly Cousins.

Mankind wasn't helping. So while The Rock struggled to defend the belt alone (and you know, he would have pulled it off, if not for interference from Triple H), Mankind sulked with his back turned to the ring. The look on Mankind's face, so sad and disappointed, in contrast to the violence behind him, was priceless. It was great theater.

The Rock and Sock Combination were history. And now Mick Foley is thinking about retirement.

It's hard to imagine The Rock ever coming up with a better partner. But a new enemy? Don't you worry about that, jabroni. In the WWF, there's always a hated rival waiting in the wings, someone else to wage war against.

CHAPTER 22
Next? The World!

What's ahead for The Rock? Everything and anything. He's already done advertisements for milk and Chef Boyardee. He's appeared on *Star Trek: Voyager* and hosted *Saturday Night Live*. He's featured in comic books, video games, and action figures. And soon, he'll be a movie star! The Rock will co-star in *The Mummy II*, alongside Brendan Fraser. He'll play a reincarnated half-man, half-scorpion! Expect to see the *The Mummy II* in theaters May 2001.

Exciting stuff, all of it, but wrestling remains his primary focus. And he's also wise enough, and modest enough (well, at least Dwayne Johnson is!), to realize that the source of his popularity is wrestling. So don't expect The Rock to turn his back on the sport, er, "sports entertainment," he loves.

The Rock concluded 1999 ranked #5 in the *Pro Wrestling Illustrated* listings. You know he'll be shooting for the top slot. *World of Wrestling* magazine recently predicted, "The Rock is on the verge of his greatest title reign ever . . . The Great One will be cooking up another championship victory."

And when you look toward wrestling in the twenty-first century, you can be sure that The Rock will be making a huge impact. His rivalry with Triple H seems to be heating up. They are similar in skills, experience, and size — and they've already waged some monstrous battles. As of April 2000, Triple H was voted the most hated wrestler in the WWF. Most popular? That would be . . . *The Rock*. Their struggle to gain power could dominate the WWF for years to come.

One thing's for certain. The future's so bright, The Rock's got to wear shades. But check him out. The Rock smells what's cooking. He's already wearing shades!

Wrestling Terms

Anklelock — A painful submission move. A wrestler twists an opponent's ankle until the opponent submits. Made famous by wrestler Ken Shamrock.

Backflip — A wrestler picks up an opponent and tosses him backward, over his head.

Bodyslam — The most common move. A wrestler picks up an opponent and slams him to the mat.

Cage Match — A match that takes place inside a steel cage with four walls but no ceiling. The winner is the first wrestler who can climb out of the cage.

Clothesline — A wrestler charges his opponent and knocks him down with an outstretched arm.

Coffin Match — Made famous by the Undertaker. The wrestler who manages to put his opponent in a coffin and close the lid wins the match.

Dropkick — A wrestler jumps into the air and kicks and opponent.

Dumpster Match — A free-for-all match in which the winning wrestler must put his opponent in a metal Dumpster and close the lid. Any items found in the Dumpster can be used to attack an opponent.

Finisher — A move perfected by a wrestler that will finish a match. For instance, the Rock's finisher is the People's Elbow. When he uses this move, the match ends.

Kick Out — A wrestler kicks out of a pin attempt before the referee counts to three.

Leg Drop — A move made famous by Hulk Hogan. While the opponent is lying on the mat, the wrestler drops a leg on the opponent's head.

Piledriver — Considered one of the deadliest wrestling moves. A wrestler holds the opponent upside down and drops the opponent on his head.

Pinned — A wrestler is pinned when his opponent manages to pin his shoulders to the mat for a three-count made by a referee.

Samoan Drop (or Backdrop) — A wrestler picks up his opponent, holds the opponent on his shoulders, and then falls backwards. The opponent hits the mat, taking the brunt of the move. A move made famous by The Rock, but used by many Samoan wrestlers.

Sharpshooter — Another painful submission move made famous by Bret Hart. A version of the Boston Crab, the wrestler grabs the opponent's legs and flips the opponent onto his stomach. Then, the wrestler sits on the opponent's back and pulls up on the opponent's legs. This stretches the opponent's legs and puts pressure on the opponent's lower back, making the opponent give up.

Sleeper Hold — A move that cuts off oxygen to a wrestler's brain, causing him to pass out.

Submission Hold — A hold designed to cause the wrestler so much pain that he gives up the match. When the wrestler taps the mat, the referee rings the bell, and the other wrestler wins.

Suplex — A wrestler raises his opponent in the air and drops him flat on his back.

A Three Way — This match boasts three men fighting at once. The first man to score a pin wins. However, when three wrestlers are fighting at once, it is very difficult for a pin to be scored.

Titleholder — A wrestler with a championship belt.

Turnbuckle — A turnbuckle is found in every corner of the ring. It holds up the ring ropes . . . but many wrestlers ram their opponent's head into the padded steel!